First published by arsEdition in 1997.
Text copyright © Jutta Langreuter
Illustrations copyright © Andrea Hebrock

First published in the UK in 2001 by
Glowworm Books Ltd. Unit 7, Greendykes Industrial Estate,
Broxburn, West Lothian, EH52 6PG, Scotland

Telephone: 01506-857570
Fax: 01506-858100
E-mail: admin@glowwormbooks.co.uk
www.glowwormbooks.co.uk

ISBN 1 871512 72 7

Printed by Proost in Belgium

UK edition edited by Lindsey Fraser

Reprint code 10 9 8 7 6 5 4 3 2 1

Roddy Rabbit's
Painted Eggs

Told by Jutta Langreuter
With illustrations by Andrea Hebrock

Glowworm Books

'Mummy!' yelled Beanie and Roddy the minute
Mummy Bunny Rabbit arrived home.
'Oh Mummy!' wailed Beanie. 'I've had a terrible day.'
'Then let's go inside and you can tell me all about it,'
said Mummy Bunny Rabbit.

'Now, tell me what happened.'
'Well, first of all, we took the egg basket and set off
to look for the hens. Just as you told us. But Roddy
kept running away - again and again!'
'I was just playing hide-and-seek,' Roddy said,
innocently.
'But it was in the forest,' Beanie yelled at him, 'so it
was very, very dangerous. Especially with all those
foxes.'
'But I was hiding from them too,' said Roddy,
'and I didn't see any foxes.'
'That's just as well,' said Mummy Bunny Rabbit.
'So what happened next?'

'When we found the hens, Roddy went right up to the cockerel and cock-a-doodle-doo-ed right in his face!' wailed Beanie.

Mummy Bunny Rabbit frowned at Roddy.

'Some of the hens laughed,' he said, cheerfully.

'But we had a terrible time trying to collect the eggs,' Beanie said, 'and the cockerel was furious.'

'Never mind,' said Mummy Bunny Rabbit, 'at least you collected some eggs in the end.'

'And then,' continued Beanie, 'when we were walking back through the forest, the basket was really, really heavy…'
'But I did help you to carry it,' added Roddy.

'When we got home, do you know what Roddy did? He took three of the eggs and tried to sit on them, like a hen! And when I tried to take them away, he screamed and screamed so loudly that the neighbours came to find out what all the noise was about.'

'I just wanted to hatch some chickens,' said Roddy.

'But rabbits don't sit on eggs. Hens sit on eggs,' Mummy told him firmly.

'It's not fair,' Roddy shouted, 'why can't I have a chicken to play with?'

'And because of all that fuss,' said Beanie, 'two of the eggs broke.'

'Oh no,' sighed Mummy Bunny Rabbit, 'whatever next?'

'I went to fetch water to boil the eggs,' said Beanie.
'And I helped too,' Roddy told her.
'Only so that you could soak me!' Beanie cried.
'Just tell me what happened,' said Mummy Bunny
Rabbit calmly.
'When the eggs had boiled, I took the paints out of
the cupboard - just as you told me - but there was no
yellow paint.'
'But I was sure that we had yellow paint,' said Mummy
Bunny Rabbit, puzzled.
'Exactly - but look around! Roddy used it all up. He
painted everything yellow - the cooker, the shelves…'
Mummy Bunny Rabbit's eyes widened with surprise.

'Doesn't it look lovely?' Roddy said, smiling.
'And then,' Beanie told her mother, 'he wasn't supposed to do any egg-painting but he insisted. Just look!'
'Oh dear, oh dear,' sighed Mummy Bunny Rabbit.

'He stole half the eggs and then he just scribbled
and scrawled on them. They are such a mess,'
Beanie moaned. She began to cry. And once she'd
begun, she couldn't stop.
'But I like painting eggs too,' Roddy wailed, 'it's
just that I can't paint very well yet.' And then he
began to cry, almost as loudly as his sister.

Just then, Daddy Bunny Rabbit came home, full of
smiles and carrying lots of delicious vegetables.
'Whatever is going on here?'
'Don't ask,' Mummy Bunny Rabbit said wearily,
'I'll tell you all about it later. Let's just make sure
that tomorrow is a much, much happier day.'

Next day Mummy Bunny Rabbit, Beanie and Roddy set off through the forest, making quite sure that no foxes saw them. When Mummy Bunny Rabbit explained what had happened to the hens, they were happy for Beanie and Roddy to collect more eggs.

At home they boiled the eggs and, once they were
ready, Mummy Bunny Rabbit gave some to Beanie to
paint. She also gave some to Roddy to paint.

Daddy Bunny Rabbit was in an excellent mood when he came home.

'What beautiful eggs,' he said, smiling. 'These really are very splendid eggs.'

Roddy looked miserable.

'What's wrong with you?' asked Daddy Bunny Rabbit.

'His eggs are not really….good enough for the Easter Bunny,' Beanie explained.

'But I think they're lovely!' said Daddy Bunny Rabbit. 'I love your eggs Beanie, and I love Roddy's eggs too. You've both painted them beautifully – just differently.'

'Daddy's absolutely right,' agreed Mummy Bunny Rabbit.

'No he's not!' moaned Beanie, 'Roddy's painting is babyish – it's not proper painting.'

'But we hide eggs at Easter for very little rabbits too, and Roddy's eggs are perfect for little rabbits,' said Daddy Bunny Rabbit.

'Do you really think so?' said Beanie. She didn't feel very sure.

'Yes, we really think so,' replied her mother, 'and we're going to hide all the eggs - yours and Roddy's.'

Roddy had a great big smile
on his face. 'I want to come
and help hide them now,' he
said delightedly.
'You do?' said Mummy Bunny
Rabbit.
'You do?' said Daddy Bunny
Rabbit.
'Of course I do!' said Roddy
Bunny Rabbit.